CATERPILLAR STEW

CATERPILLAR STEW

A Feast of Animal Poems
from Gavin Ewart

Illustrated by Ronald Ferns

HUTCHINSON
London   Sydney   Auckland   Johannesburg

First published in Great Britain in 1990 by Hutchinson Children's Books
An imprint of The Random Century Group Ltd
20 Vauxhall Bridge Road, London SW1V 2SA

Random Century Australia (Pty) Ltd
88–91 Albion Street, Surry Hills, NSW 2010

Random Century New Zealand Ltd
32–34 View Road, PO Box 40–086, Glenfield, Auckland 10

Random Century Hutchinson South Africa (Pty) Ltd
PO Box 337, Bergvlei 2012, South Africa

Printed and bound in Great Britain by
Butler and Tanner Ltd,
Frome and London

British Library Cataloguing in Publication Data
Ewart, Gavin, *1916–*
Caterpillar stew.
I. Title   II. Ferns, Ronald
821.912

ISBN 0-09-174097-5

The Little Cat in
Putney

(Tune: *The Yellow Rose of Texas*)

There's a little cat in Putney
That means a lot to me,
I think that he's the nicest
That you could ever see –

A lovely little tabby,
And white, pure white, his paws.
He has the whitest shirt-front
And that's all right because

He's the sweetest little fellow
That anyone could know,
His eyes are bright and shiny,
He's always purring so.

You can talk of tigers all you want,
And leopards wild and free –
But that little cat in Putney
Is the only cat for me!

Introduction

We share the world with the animals. Like us, they live and die on the same earth. As Noah might have said, as he sailed away in the Ark: 'We're all in the same boat!'

Noah was the first ecologist. According to the old story in the Bible, he saved all the existing species of his time. We should try to do the same.

These poems pay tribute to the beauty and variety of the creatures with whom we share the planet. They are meant to tell you something about them, as well as being entertaining. A special section has been devoted to the amazing animals of Australia.

Eat Up Your Insects!

Do you fancy a nice caterpillar stew?
Or would fried locusts appeal?
Is a toasted beetle the thing for you?
Would some spiders make a nice meal?

Worms are all protein, and oak-tree grubs
Are lovely when fed on flour,
And just as good as the chips in pubs
For promoting muscular power!

Cockroaches curried, or silk-worm crisps,
Termites with woodlouse sauce?
You won't end up starving will o' the wisps
If you eat a large insect course!

Ants are the poor man's caviare –
On bread, they've a peppery taste.
So eat up your insects, for there they are,
Don't let them all go to waste!

Note: All these insects have been eaten by human beings, and many still are. The Romans loved oak-tree grubs; Aristotle, the great Greek philosopher, liked cicadas. In the 1960s an English tramp told Colin McInnes about the joys of eating ants. A locust contains about 42.76% protein and 6.50% fat – nearly as nourishing as red meat.

The Oyster

The Oyster is a selfish shellfish —
It keeps itself to itself.
It lives alone and self-contained
On a shallow coastal shelf.

The Stick Insect

The Stick Insect
Isn't a thick insect.
It's very hard to spot it.
If you want perfect camouflage
It's got it!

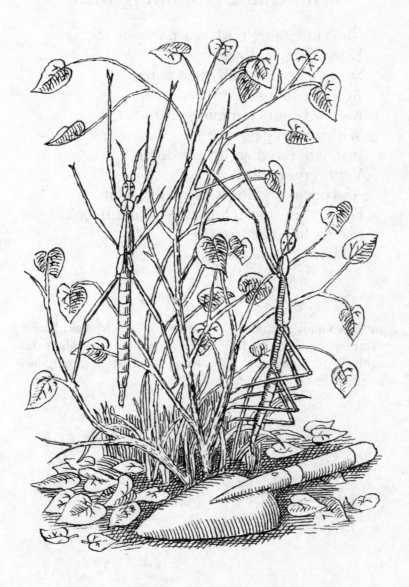

The Giant Humming-bird

Most humming-birds when they're taking
Honey from a flower
Stay still by agitating their wings
At tremendous speed.
But the Giant Humming-bird,
With amazing power,
Just flaps its wings up and down
Very very slowly,
And opens and shuts its tail like a fan.
Darwin was the first to take a careful look.
It's less like a helicopter
And more like a rook.

Note: The Giant Humming-bird (*Patagona gigas*) was observed by Darwin in Chile in 1835. It is 5–6 ins. from bill to tail, roughly eight times the size of the smallest humming-bird, which is about ¾ in. long.

The Bat

Consider the Bat.
You'd think it would be good at cricket,
With a name like *that* –
But it never scores a run, or takes a
    wicket,
Though its trajectory is terrifically fast
    and flat!

15

Frogs Are Free

Cats have cat fleas,
Dogs have dog fleas,
American pigs have
Hog fleas.

Bats have bat fleas.
Hedgehogs have hedgehog fleas.
But whoever heard of frogs having
Frog fleas?

Note: Pigs are always called hogs in the United States.

Caterpillars and Boxes

The red things that stand about in streets,
That people put letters into,
Are called Pillar Boxes.

When I was young I kept Caterpillars
In cardboard boxes with air-holes in the lids –
You might have called them
Caterpillar Boxes!

The Wren

The Wren is the smallest British bird –
Or hadn't you heard?

Sheepshape

A Sheep is sheepshape,
A ship can be shipshape.
But if a Frenchman said
A sheep is sheepshape
Would he mean
'A Sheep is sheepshape'
Or 'A ship is shipshape'?

Note: When sailors say something is 'shipshape' they mean that
it is all in order and under control.

Water Voles and Moles

Water Voles
Are quite different from Moles.
They have different roles.
They live on river banks in holes,
They can swim like soles.

A Mole, in water, cannot manoeuvre.
He's more like a subterranean Hoover,
A kind of underground earth-mover.

Cats

When it comes to Cats,
I don't like the aristocrats!
I have an aversion
To the pampered Persian.
The ones with bad-tempered faces,
Who despise the inferior races,
May be gorgeously fluffy –
But they *look* mean and huffy!

The Lark

Why do they say, 'What a lark!'?
A Lark isn't jolly.
It never giggles or titters,
It flies straight up from the ground and twitters.
It isn't a practical joker
And its face is as straight as a poker!

A Nose is a Nose is a Nose

The Proboscis Monkey
Looks like a lot of people
I could mention –
But the male's big nose
Is mainly there
To attract the female's attention!

The Yapok or Water-opossum

In the mountains
From Guatemala to Southern Brazil –
Lives the marsupial Yapok,
With a smell that makes you quite ill.
It's very seldom seen and the locals
(When they think of it at all)
Think of it as an Otter.
Obviously, it's a bit of a rotter.

The Rhyming Likes and Dislikes of the Lamb

The Lamb
Doesn't like being rhymed with 'jam' and 'ham'
Or 'yam', 'pram' and 'Wham!',
Or even with 'cryptogram' or 'parallelogram' –
But more with out-of-the-way things like a door
    'jamb',
A 'choriamb' or a 'dithyramb'.
There's really no telling
How terribly hot a Lamb is on spelling!

The Scorpion

Always bend over backwards
To avoid the Scorpion,
As it bends over *forwards*
To get at *you*!
The place where a Scorpion lives
Is always a torrid one –
Don't go to such places
Or your death will be a horrid one!

The Brontosaurus

There aren't enough words in any
Dictionary or thesaurus
To describe the mating of the
Brontosaurus!
Not even a Dictionary of Quotations
Can do justice to the weighty implications.

The Meerkats of Africa

Meerkats go about in packs,
They don't hang loose –
They're not really *cats* at all,
But more a mongoose.
They have great capabilities,
Make no mistake,
A Meerkat can kill a scorpion
Or even a snake.
They rescue each others' children
And have lookouts when they're feeding
And a system of babysitters –
The kind of co-operation
That the human race is needing!

Note: David Attenborough's BBC programme *Meerkats United* is my source for all these facts. I'm not sure whether the young ones are called 'Meerkittens' or not.

Love for Predators

It's the Carnivores of Britain
By whom my heart is smitten!
I am clawed and scratched and bitten
By all their scaly, beaky, toothy jaws,
Their furry arms and clutching claws!
What mercy can they show or give –
Since they have to eat to live?

The Coelacanth

The Coelacanth has a hollow spine
Quite a lot like yours and mine –
A prehistoric kind of fish,
Dead as anyone could wish,
They reckoned. Quite extinct. Until
They trawled one up, alive, not ill
But in the very best of health,
In 1938. By stealth
Nature plays tricks on scientists.
She tweaks their noses, slaps their wrists.
And no one knows, it seems to me,
What's at the bottom of the sea!

Note: The first live coelacanth of modern times was netted in the Indian Ocean off East London, South Africa, in 1938. This fish has changed very little, the experts say, since its first appearance. It has been found as a fossil in Upper Devonian rocks, millions of years old.

The Mynah Bird

There's no finer bird
Than the Mynah Bird.
It certainly can talk!
It can say, 'Oh, rather!'
Or, 'How's your father?'
Or, 'Would you like to come for a walk?'

Nobody chatters
On secret matters.
It repeats all it hears.
If you don't want a riot
It's best to stay quiet –
A Mynah Bird is all ears.

Mice and Cricket

If Mice played cricket
You would see a batsmouse
Standing at the wicket
Surrounded by fieldsmice
(Who might or might not be Field Mice).
Would this be confusing
Or very, very nice?

Note:
Call him
A fieldsman or a fielder –
It really doesn't matter –
But a batsman in cricket
Can't be called a batter.

The Crab

Round the shores of Great Britain,
If you meet a Crab,
He will be reddish and brownish
And rather drab.
But if in the Pacific Ocean
You meet one big crab-fellow,
He may be in parts red and blue
And very bright yellow.
He may live on Christmas Island
Or have sticking-out moveable eyes –
Land Crabs of the South Atlantic
Are quite a surprise.

Extinct

Deadly Jurassic Dinosaurs,
Cretaceous Crocodiles,
And pleasure-loving Plesiosaurs
Have gone away. It's miles
Back in the past! We find
Just nothing of them but the bones
That they have left behind.

First bird, the Archaeopteryx,
He's nowhere to be found,
Finished with helicopterics,
Stunt-flier gone to ground!
O Allosaurs, Tyrannosaurs,
All gone – and just as well, I think –
The greedy carnivores!

Mild, leaf-eating Iguanodons!
And Pterodactyls too
(The cousins of Pteranodons),
The leather birds that flew,
Don't fill the modern sky,
No Brontosaurs block motorways,
We've missed them, you and I!

Now we, with all benevolence,
Should treasure what we've got –
The Rhinos, Tigers, Elephants.
What's left is not a lot.
Don't hunt them! Poacher's pay
Will never get them back again!
Not ever! No! No way!

The Toxodon

Imagine if you can a gigantic rat
As big as an elephant –
With its teeth it could gnaw
The biggest tree you ever saw.

That was the Toxodon,
Millions of years ago, in Argentina.
If you've ever seen a
Creature like that it must have been a
Very bad dream or delirium!
It lived at the same time as the Megatherium,
A huge, heavy giant sloth.
No living person has ever seen
One or the other or both.

The Toxodon was able to swim –
It really *was* an elephant-sized water rat –
And what could be more terrifying than *that*?

The Snow Leopard

All Snow Leopards are whitish grey
And live to the North of the Himalayas,
The mountain slopes are their fields of play
And they are the most sure-footed players.
Their bodies have dark rosettes or rings
And plumelike fur, among other things.
All small beasts, and mountain deer,
Regard the Snow Leopard with fear.
Because they're eight feet long, you see,
The body's five, the tail is three!

Safe

If you live in the middle of Birmingham
You won't be destroyed by a Shark,
No Octopus will bother you
If you have a tent in Hyde Park.

If you live in a boat in a distant sea
No Lion will bite you up,
As far as Tigers are concerned
You'll be safer than tea in a cup.

If you fear sea animals, stick to land —
That's the everlasting rule.
Land animals don't swim much in the sea —
A Wolf in the waves feels a fool!

The Ways of the Lobster

The Lobster
Is not a criminal, a gangster, or a mobster.
He doesn't walk crooked like the crab.
In all that righteous armour-plate
He walks quite straight.

The Robin

The Robin looks a happy, cheerful little bird,
The joy of the Christmas Card.
But Robins, in fact, are dedicated fighters
And a Robin's life is hard.
They fight each other, for territory or courtship,
And peck out each other's eyes,
Or starve to death in the freezing winter.
That Christmas Card tells lies.

Buffaloes and Bisons

In America,
If you hear a heavy pounding galloping,
It's a herd of Buffalo.

In Europe,
If you hear a heavy pounding galloping,
It's a herd of Bison.

They both look very alike.
Patchy and shaggy and as if they were moulting.

In zoos they stand about,
Lonely and missing their friends in the herd –
They can look very moth-eaten.

The Elephant-shrew

The Elephant-shrew
Is less like an Elephant
Than me and you.
It's only a few centimetres long,
It can't perform in circuses
Or move trees
Or go down on its knees.

It's smaller than a rat
And much smaller than a chipmunk –
It's only called the Elephant-shrew
Because some bright person
Thought its nose looked like a trunk!

The Bobcat

No matter what the Bobcat thinks,
In reality it's a short-haired Lynx.
It will eat anything alive,
Mate with domestic cats,
And it's very dangerous and aggressive.
It's never averse to a fight,
It will attack human beings on sight.
In the USA and Mexico
Its presence is excessive.

Destroying the Planet

Nature isn't just 'beautiful' –
The Butterfly and the Rose –
Everything feeds on something else,
That's the way it goes!

But conscienceless, omnivorous Man
Is the one we should be booing,
Because he's the only animal
That really knows what it's doing.

The Alpaca

They talk about pulling the wool
Over somebody's eyes –
The Alpaca looks as though it's been able to pull
An old tatty ragged matted rug
Over its head, its body, and even its thighs.
If it lay flat on a living room floor
That would be a complete disguise!

Note: 'To pull the wool over somebody's eyes' means to deceive them.

The Alpaca is a kind of Llama, famous for its wool, bred for centuries by the natives of South America. It can be red, brown, white or black. It is descended from the Guanaco, the Wild Llama, that lives in herds in the mountains and plains.

The Horse-fly

Have you ever seen a Horse fly?
The Greeks had a winged horse called Pegasus
In their old fairy stories —
But he only existed in their imagination.

Unfortunately, the horrible Horse-fly
Does exist, one of Nature's nastiest legacies
To us, not one of her glories!
And his sharp sting is a *real* irritation!

Highland Cattle

The pride of Scotland, see the Highland Cattle!
They're calm and wise and above the battle.
Like old gentlemen in brown tweed suits,
That seem quite comfortable and baggy,
They stand in that misty romantic landscape
And look shaggy!

Marcus, the Masterful Millipede

Marcus, the Masterful Millipede,
Was in some ways a bit of a silly pede.
He was always boasting and telling the centipedes
That he had ten times more feet –
He called them incomplete –
But in fact they had more than enough for their needs.

With only *two*, people like you and me
Can get from A to B.

Gondwanaland

O take me back to Gondwanaland
Before the Terrible Split
When what is now cloven
Was all interwoven
And didn't differ a bit!

O dinosaurs of Gondwanaland,
Now so vanished away,
I miss you sorely,
I ache so rawly,
Won't you come back one day?

Marsupials of Gondwanaland,
Bigger than elephants too,
Sloths and possums,
Odontoglossums,
Why do I dream of you?

Steamy heat of Gondwanaland,
When reptiles were the kings!
Life's so mammalian
And neo-Australian
And lots of *un*pleasant things!

O waft me back to Gondwanaland,
Fly me away in the sky –
For ever I'm all
In thrall to what's primal,
Until the day that I die!

Note: Millions of years ago, South America, Africa and
Australia were all one huge mass of land – known now as
Gondwana. When they drifted apart, the three continents each
took with them their own animals. Australia, for example, has
animals that are found nowhere else in the world.

Odontoglossums are orchids.

DOWN UNDER

Down Under

(Australia, Tasmania, New Zealand)

Kookaburras and Currawongs
Throng the Antipodes,
There are seas with Sharks
And Wild Life Parks
And Parrots among the trees.
The Sulphur-Crested Cockatoo
Keeps a beady eye on you!

Dingo Dogs and Platypi
Ply the unlettered plain,
Dark Manatees
Swim Northern seas,
There's too much Sugar Cane.
Spiny Anteaters abound –
Not so nice to have around!

Wallabies and Kangaroos
Choose the wide open space
That the farmers keep
For flocks of sheep.
Grass vanishes without trace.
Ma is marsupial, Phascogales
Leave the sea to playful Whales.

Wombats wander and dig holes
Moles might think were nice.
At such low levels
Tasmanian Devils
Burrow – take my advice,
Avoid the deadly Thylacine
And be in bed by half past nine!

Emus with their gangling knees
Please hardly anyone!
They look like thugs,
With ugly mugs
Most foul beneath the sun!
The Kiwi, though, without a tail,
Is lovable and like a Quail!

The Duck-billed Platypus

The Duck-billed Platypus
Can't be considered an Alien –
But it's very primitive
And a perfect Australian.
If it ever spoke to anyone
It would speak in old-fashioned Australian slang:
'She's apples!', 'Don't come the raw prawn with me!'
It's the only mammal that lays eggs*.
It swims marvellously and scuttles about
On very short legs.

Note: *Except for the Spiny Anteater, also known as the Echidna. The Platypus (Ornithorhynchus) was once known as the Duck-mole. When a specimen was first sent to Europe it was regarded as a joke; nobody could believe that the body was not the work of a hoaxer. 'She's apples!' (now a rather out-of-date expression) means 'It's fine!' 'Don't come the raw prawn with me!' means 'Don't try to con me! (I wasn't born yesterday).'

The Koala

In its native land the Koala
Is never called a Koala *Bear*;
That would be unfair
Because it isn't a bear.
In their accuracy
The Australians have far outstripped us.
It's a nocturnal marsupial that eats eucalyptus.

Galàhs

The most beautiful grey and pink parrots are called
    Galàhs –
All of them rhyme (more or less) with 'bazaars'.
Australians regard them as silly. They go about in
    flocks.
You won't see them in Sydney, down at the docks.
They're not townbirds at all – they're of another
    persuasion –
And people will say, as a joke: 'It was a Galàh
    Occasion!'
Though Gala Occasions must be very rare in *their*
    lives,
Since they don't drink beer or have Golden Weddings
    or wives!

The Soldier Crab

The Soldier Crab, solemn, sedate,
Unlike all others, walks quite straight.

Note: The Soldier Crab is a large Australian land crab, bluish-
grey in colour.

Emus

Emus
Aren't cosy British birds like Robins and Seamews.
They are very ugly and greedy,
They will steal from the poor and needy,
They look like the demons in old Italian paintings.
Such as could cause heart attacks and faintings.

Note: 'Seamew' is a rather old-fashioned name for the ordinary
Gull. Emus are quite capable of stealing steaks from a barbecue.

The Funnel-web Spider

If you're in the outback,
In Australia,
You must watch out for the Funnel-web Spider –
It isn't one of the boys, it's a rank outsider!

As you sit on the toilet, the lavatory, the loo
Or, as Australians call it, the dunnee,
If it bites you it isn't funny!
The bite of the Funnel-web spider
Won't just tickle you or thrill you –
It's very likely to kill you!

The Broad-footed Phascogales

Mouse-sized, mouse-shaped, with tapering tails,
They have very small big-toes without nails.
They are never seen wearing shoes or socks,
They can climb easily up trees and rocks –
Some species can run across a cave roof upside down.
They have a white underside but their top's reddish-
  brown.

Note: Found in Australia and New Guinea, and known as
Kangaroo-mice.

The Numbat

Everyone knows almost everything about the
  Wombat
But almost nobody has ever even heard of the
  Numbat.
It will eat termites by the pint and the litre –
In fact it's an exclusive termite-eater.

It's a beautiful, delicate, quick little animal
With a long sticky tongue, an Australian marsupial,
Flat-headed, bushy-tailed – you will find it here and
  there
In the south of Australia, but it's getting very rare.

The Muttonbird of New Zealand

The Muttonbird is really called a Sooty Shearwater.
It eats nothing but fish. It doesn't fear water.
It dives right in. When people kill it
They put it under the grill and grill it,
And its horrible fatty stench will be adorning
Their kitchens for weeks, both night and morning.
It's the terrible fishy taste and the *smell*
That makes all sensitive New Zealanders scream and
  yell!

Fairy Penguins

Fairy Penguins are also called Little Penguins –
Australia's only penguins, the only ones.
They wait till dark, then come ashore to roost,
Wading through the surf, crossing the beach,
Whole families, fathers, mothers, daughters, sons.

Note: Fairy Penguins, the only penguins in Australia, live in
burrows or crevices in the cliffs or sand dunes of Gabo Island, St
Helens Island and Phillip Island. They are the smallest penguins
in the world.

Myrtle, the Pig-nosed Turtle

Meet Myrtle,
The Pig-nosed Turtle!
Underneath the Australian sun
She has a lot of Australian fun.
If you're outgoing and outgiving
Even a very ugly person
Can get a lot of joy
Out of living!

The Kookaburra

The Kookaburra can't be found
In the London Underground.
The Kookaburra flies out free
Where the gum's the only tree.
It has befoozled us and flipped us
In the Land of Eucalyptus,
Far from City fraud and fracas.
It *can* be called The Laughing Jackass.

Bilbies

You'll never see a Bilby
Wearing a trilby –
It doesn't, either, ever wear a suit.
Its true name is the Rabbit-eared Bandicoot.
Far from the cities, in the deserts of Australia,
It lives in burrows, one of the prettiest of the
    mammalia.
Soft blue-grey fur and engaging ways.
For the Bilbies, naturalists have nothing but
    praise!

The Spotted Dasyure

The Spotted Dasyure or Australian Native Cat
Is a marsupial carnivore and none the worse for that.
It spends all day curled up asleep in holes.
At night it hunts small animals. It would eat voles
If there were any voles in Australia. A cat of another
 kidney
Is the Eastern Native Cat, which is common around
 Sydney.
It walks about respected, wherever it chooses to go,
But it has no raised pads on the soles of its feet, and
 no big-toe.

The Bowerbird

The male Bowerbird builds complicated bowers
Of twigs and sticks, mosses, fruit and flowers.
He will hang around near them for hours and
    hours.

When a female flies by he starts his song and dance,
Hopping from side to side, retreat and then
    advance.
This, for him, is courtship – to beguile, to entrance!

He's a true Don Juan, the bower's there for one
    reason:
To woo as many females as possible in the mating
    season!

Dunnarts, Dibblers and the Honey Possum

Among the Antechinuses and Dunnarts, the Dibbler
Is as large as a small rat but it isn't a nibbler.
It goes after insects but it also likes nectar –
And so does the Western Pygmy Possum, in the same
    sector.
In the Australian heathland, though, you can't beat a
Little Honey Possum as a nectar and honey eater!
Doesn't eat insects, has no teeth, a long tongue. It's
    one happy possum
If you let it alone to probe the nectar-filled Banksia
    blossom!

The Frilled Lizard

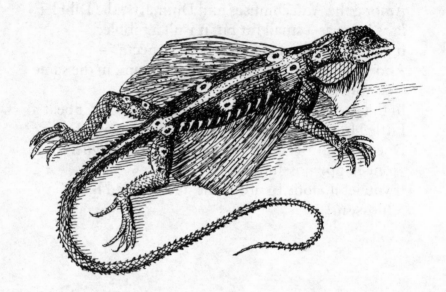

The Frilled Lizard lives mostly in trees –
Insects and small vertebrates are on its menu.
It keeps alive easily on these,
But if you meet it at some unexpected venue
It will open its mouth and try to scare you.
Find one, and see – in fact, I dare you!

Note: The Frilled Lizard is Australia's best-known reptile; but,
since it's only 22 cm long (though the tail is 44 cm) it isn't very
frightening.

The Squid and the Blue-ringed Octopus

The Squid
Is not a desirable present
For any kind of kid –
But one should make more of a fuss
Over the Blue-ringed Octopus.
It's more poisonous than might be reckoned,
It can kill crabs and large fish in 30 seconds.

Note: The Blue-ringed Octopus is one of the most famous inhabitants of the seas round Australia. It can produce, at will, the blue rings on its tentacles that warn other creatures of its poisonous nature. It's one of the most venomous sea animals. Although it measures only 20 cm (less than 8 ins) from one tentacle tip to another, it can kill crabs and fish much larger than itself in 30 seconds.

The Modesty of Australian Dinosaurs

Australian Dinosaurs
Didn't throw their bones about
Like the big brash American kind –
In fact, in most cases,
A fossilized footprint
Is all you'll ever find!

Malas and Bilbies and Woylies and Quolls

Malas and Bilbies and Woylies and Quolls
All work in Australia and never have hols.
They are the pride and the joy of the nation
And a permanent reason for Celebration!

Note: The Mala is the Rufous Hare Wallaby, the Bilby is the
Rabbit-eared Bandicoot, the Woylie is the Bush-tailed Bettong.
There are different kinds of Quoll; the Spotted Tail Quoll is
known as the Tiger Cat, one of the last of Australia's marsupial
predators.

Roos v. Wedge-tailed Eagles

What would you do
If you were a very young
Red, Western Grey or Tree Kangaroo?
Just as hares avoid the beagles
You'd avoid the Wedge-tailed Eagles!

Note: The Great Grey Kangaroo was discovered by Captain
Cook in 1770. This was the first time it had ever been seen by a
white man. Beagles are the dogs used for hunting hares.

The Sand Monitor

The Sand Monitor, or Gould's Goanna,
Lives in the desert in a fearsome manner.
It can grow to 1.6 metres
And it's one of the most dedicated eaters
Of insects, birds, carrion and mammals –
Though perhaps it draws the line at Camels.
It is completely *compos mentis*
And knows where the smallest trace of scent is –
And so do its 2-metre relatives, the Perenties!

Note: People say there are 30,000 camels in Australia. The first 33 were imported from India by Burke and Wills for their explorations in 1860.

Compos mentis means 'sane'. The Sand Monitor has a special organ, known as Jacobson's Organ, which can detect the slightest hint of a smell.

The Great Karnivorous
Kangaroo in 1988

They thought it might have existed
But no one knew how or why
And all their theories were twisted
Until this very July.

But now at Riversleigh, Queensland,
They've found a mean skull beneath.
In that fossil-deposit has-beens' land,
With horrible steak-knife teeth!

Five feet tall, Ekaltadeta,
And twenty million years old,
A killer roo too, a flesh-eater,
A bounder, quite beastly and bold!

Note: The first complete skull of Ekaltadeta was discovered by Dr Michael Archer in July 1988. Modern kangaroos are all herbivores – grass-eaters. 'Carnivorous' means flesh-eating (the K in the title is a joke).

The Spotted Cuscus

Elephants can be terrible tuskers,
Street musicians are noisy buskers –
But quiet . . . calm . . . slow
Is the Spotted Cuscus!

It looks half-witted and even loopy. All
The same it's a prize Marsupial!

Note: The Spotted Cuscus, with the possums, lives in the highest branches of the forests of Papua New Guinea and Northern Australia. It eats fruit, flowers and leaves.

Muttaburrasaurus

Raise a paean of praise!
Sing in zestful chorus!
In honour of a great Australian dinosaur –
Muttaburrasaurus!
Thirty-four feet long and weighed a ton,
It was a big plant-eating Iguanodon!

Note: A 'paean' is a song of praise and rejoicing. The
Muttaburrasaurus was called by this name because its remains
were first discovered at Muttaburra.

Australia!

Australian animals
Haunt my dreams –
They're old-fashioned
As chocolate creams!

Furry animals
That lay eggs,
Odd as a kitchen chair
With six legs!

Mansized creatures
Born inches long!
Koala, Bunyip,
Billabong!

There's outback magic
Everywhere,
In *pouches* babies
Sit and stare!

And in the hot parts
All one meets
Is: Parrots, Cockatoos,
Lorikeets!

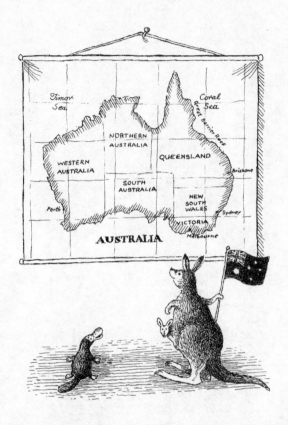

Note: This poem is about the Duck-billed Platypus, the Kangaroo, and Marsupials and Parrots in general. When a Kangaroo is first born it is very small indeed. Bunyips are ghostlike monsters. They are supposed to live in billabongs, which are pools or ponds. These are both words used by the Aboriginals, the first inhabitants of Australia.

77

Contents